Assassin's Love

CHRIS NEO

CCNG Ltd
T/A CCNG PUBLISHINGS
Unit 3 Gateway Mews, Ringway, Bounds Green
London, N11 2UT, UK

www.ccngpublishings.com
Author: www.chris-neo.com

All correspondence to: enquiries@ccngpublishings.com

Dedication

To those who love!

Note to Reader

This is a work of fiction. Though I adore literary writing, I do not write in high literary style, but rather with emotion-filled dialogue. Every sentence is part of the story and moves the plot forward.

When I read a book, I am impatient. I do not want to read ten pages if only two sentences move the story forward. So my dear reader, be prepared for a fast-moving tale.

I hope you enjoy this short love story!

Subscribe to the email list and discussion groups:
www.chris-neo.com/subscribe
www.facebook.com/ChrisNeo1010
Twitter: @ChrisNeo1010

One

Valentino marvelled at several items on display at the gypsy kiosk. Their tags read: Assassin's pancakes, Assassin's jams, Gypsy Assassin's pastries, and Assassin's pink juice.

The bazaar was packed this sunny Saturday, the first day of spring, though he spied a few sparse patches of snow clinging to life in the side alleys. The buzz of merchants hawking their wares rivalled that of the shoppers' euphoria, all mingling, laughing and making jokes.

Valentino motioned his gorgeous wife, Heleanne, to step up beside him. Her blonde hair glistened in the mid-morning rays. She was trim and fit for her forty years. He'd always appreciated the energy of a younger woman, though ten years felt less different now than it had when they were first wed.

Across from them, a dark-haired gypsy with wide black eyes touched one of the items Valentino had just been considering. The lady was flanked by two swarthy men, while a second much older gypsy woman clung to the shadows behind them.

"Best Assassin's pancakes," she said, meeting Valentino's eyes. "Gives you double the energy."

He noted the scar running from cheek to ear on her left side. It belied the warm, sweet smile and lithe dancer's body. This was not merely a beautiful face with black velvet hair. This was a woman with a past. She wet her lips which captured his gaze once more.

Valentino rubbed a hand over his waistline. "Pastries and sugar… they all pile up here."

Seemingly out of nowhere she extended a jar to him. "Refreshing Assassin's lemonade then."

A flutter of fabric brushed across the back of his hand. Heleanne walked past him to examine items on a side shelf.

Smiling, Valentino explained, "Ah, that would send me to the bathroom all night long, I'm afraid."

The two men shared a chuckle from their positions at her side.

"I see," the raven-haired beauty said, and instead swept over and picked up the item Heleanne had in her sights. "If you have that problem, then you must have our Assassin's pink juice."

"And what is that made of?" he asked, playing along.

"Top secret family recipe," she replied swifty. "But I can tell you this juice eliminates the need for those annoying nightly interruptions. Not only that…" She leaned closer to him, tipping forward to expose the fleshy expanse barely concealed by her bodice. In a whisper she added, "It also refreshes the parts that other juices cannot reach. Double the benefits!"

Valentino raised an eyebrow, unable to disguise his interest in the woman herself, or the promise her unspoken words conveyed.

The older gypsy woman mysteriously appeared at Valentino's side. "Wild berries and rare herbs," she spoke in low, accented tones. "If you notice no gain, you bring it back tomorrow… full refund. No questions asked!"

Valentino could smell the garlic on the old woman's breath, but he instead addressed his question to the younger beauty in front of him. "How do I know you will be here tomorrow?"

She gave a beguiling smile. "We just arrived. We will stay at least through the end of spring."

"Do not forget," the old woman's voice rattled. "It refresh the parts no other juice can reach… or your money back."

Valentino forced his gaze to shift to the old gypsy at his side, then to return to the younger woman facing him for confirmation.

She nodded with a soft smile, then produced a small plastic cup into which she poured a sample of the juice. "Try it. Feel the effect."

Cup in hand, Valentino was still leary, but seeing no opposition from his wife who had busied herself looking at items near the taller of the two gypsy men, he took a sip.

The taste was neither sweet nor bitter, but he felt a tingle as it travelled down his throat to his belly. Did he detect a sparkle in the old woman's eyes?

With determination, he swigged the rest of the sample and handed the cup back to the dark-haired lady. She held forth the rest of the bottle which Valentino accepted. Then he reached into his pocket and withdrew a folded stack of bills. With the bottle weighing heavily in his other hand, he offered the money to the old gypsy lady, inviting her to take payment.

She extracted two of the largest denominations from the money clip before handing it back.

Valentino laughed. "But you have taken double of what your price tag says."

"That fee is without guarantee," she warbled. "With money back, the price is double!"

Hearing the tinkle of the younger woman's laughter, he joined in the merriment with his own snicker and pocketed the rest of his cash. His sight fell once more on the bosom of the lovely lady before him. He bowed a silent thanks.

"Mmm…" came the sound of his wife's voice. He turned to see her tasting one of the Assassin's pancakes, and watched as she paid the taller gypsy man a not insignificant amount of money.

Valentino assessed the man. Early thirties, ruddy complexion, chiselled muscles. No doubt the traveller's life demanded physical activities that kept him fit.

"Are you assassins, then?" he heard Heleanne's throaty voice inquire.

The man erected himself to his full height, then bent at the waist to capture and kiss Heleanne's hand. "My name is Alexi."

Valentino thanked the older gypsy woman while watching the others from the corner of his eye.

His wife was flirting openly now, her lips slightly parted as she gazed up at Alexi with a challenge. "You didn't answer my question."

Valentino resisted the urge to flinch when the old gypsy woman clutched at his free hand and rubbed it between her two rough palms.

Alexi again bent forward, this time to whisper something in Heleanne's ear.

With a playful smile his wife asked the man, "And who do you assassinate?"

Alexi's expression turned serious, his voice low and conspiratorial. "For the right price… anyone a client wants."

Valentino stepped back abruptly, dislodging his hand from the old gypsy's clutches. Then he moved quickly towards Heleanne. "Mr. Alexi," he began, pulling the remaining cash out of his pocket. "Is this enough to assassinate my wife?"

The taller man's brows wrinkled. "Your wife is so beautiful," he replied, again reaching for Heleanne's hand, now staring deeply into her eyes. "It would cost you all your wealth!"

Pocketing his exposed cash, Valentino rasped, "Maybe this is all I am worth. At least in terms of money."

Heleanne simply giggled like a schoolgirl, enchanted by the foreigner. "How much to assassinate my husband, dear Alexi?"

The gypsy man's intent stare never left Heleanne's face. "For you, gorgeous beauty, I would do it for free. You will be my prize."

Valentino laughed out load. "Now that is a fair exchange!" Then he added in an undertone, "Be careful what you wish for."

The old gypsy woman suddenly appeared beside Heleanne. She had a way of moving that evaded observation and it flustered Valentino. "What is your name, beautiful lady?" she asked his wife.

"Heleanne," came the answer, along with the reddening of her cheeks.

"So you are both hell and Ann?" The older woman's brows arched. "Give me your hand."

Without Heleanne's compliance, the old lady grasped his wife's hand between her calloused ones, much as she had done with Valentino. But this time after taking stock of the soft skin, she turned Heleanne's palm face up in front of her eyes.

"For sure, I see hell and Anne here." Pointing to the younger gypsy lady, she added, "We have your match. This one behind me is called Holly Ann."

Valentino noted how the old woman's words affected the raven-haired beauty. He detected a visible ruffle, as if she wanted to shake something off of her.

"Holly Ann transfers people to the holy world," the old gypsy concluded.

"Well, Holly Anna," Valentino trilled. "Are you an assassin, too?"

Again a shiver cascaded through her body, but this time she raised herself up proudly. "My true name is Rafaella. And my *cousin* Alexi was joking. Of course we are not assassins. We are merchants, as you can see."

Sharp, quiet words practically hissed from the elder lady's lips. "Why have you given your real name?"

Rafaella shrugged.

"There is always more to what the eye can see." Valentino intentionally angled himself to block Rafaella's view of his wife, which also had the effect of shielding his own expression from Heleanne.

"You are new in our market," he heard his wife whisper to Alexi. He could imagine her subtle smile and the way her lips would curl. "How long are you staying?"

"Who knows?" the old woman's answer interrupted everyone's daydreams. "A day, a week, a month, a season, a year? Depends on sales of product… *and services.*"

As if without thought, Heleanne's question followed immediately. "What services?"

Valentino did not miss the acute squinting of one eye before the old gypsy hag replied, "We have many skills… household services, therapeutic remedies… even permanent resolutions to many issues. If you have a requirement, just ask and we will tell you if we can provide such a service."

Raising his bottle of Assassin's pink juice in a kind of goodbye salute, Valentino took Heleanne by the arm and began to lead her away, calling behind him, "I'll be back tomorrow to get my refund!"

Two

Helanne made a show of opening and closing the refrigerator without removing anything, then doing something similar with all the cupboards. Finally she turned to her husband and huffed, "I need some items from the market. I've decided to cook you something special for dinner tonight."

She did not even wait for his reply before gathering her purse and taking to the streets. She headed straight for Alexi and the gypsy stall.

The same four staff members were present this day. Heleanne took pleasure that Rafaella and the old hag looked deep in discussion with an older male customer. Sidling up to Alexi, she asked him sweetly for another Assassin's pancake.

"It seems you found something to your liking, miss." He took his time lifting the fluffy pancake from the tray, placing it on a napkin, and raising it toward Heleanne's awaiting lips.

She accepted the treat, taking a first bite, and then inclining her head in the direction of a side alley. Heleanne took four steps away and then nodded to indicate Alexi should follow.

She did not notice his exchange of glances with the older gypsy woman before he set out in the same direction.

It took only moments for Alexi to catch up with Heleanne where she had paused at the corner of a side street just out of sight of the gypsy stand.

"I need some of your services," she cooed charmingly.

"What are you after, gorgeous lady?"

"You know how to compliment a woman. Fearless, even in front of my husband yesterday." Heleanne looked to either side to see if anyone was watching, then returned her full attention to the muscular foreigner. "For starters, let's say I find you handsome as well. My husband is old. We no longer have intimate relations."

Alexi took half a step backwards. "I liked you from the first moment, but that is not a service I provide for pay."

"Oh, I don't wish to pay for intimacy," Heleanne assured him, reaching to place her palm along the length of his cheek.

Alexi's brown eyes drilled her with intensity. "Think twice. Do you not have another agenda in mind?"

Heleanne nodded, amused. "Let's get to know each other a bit first."

"What payable service are you really after, lady?"

She felt the stubble of his beard against her hand. "Can you escape for a short while? Walk me to my house," she suggested. "It's not far."

Alexi claimed her hand and held it fast, then nodded his agreement.

Heleanne took them on a casual stroll through the city streets, ending up next to the bank of a small stream. In the distance stood a big home with a small tower on one side. "This is my house."

"Aristocratic and beautiful like you!" Alexi complimented.

"My husband is nothing but a peasant," she replied. "He used to be handsome and active. But he came into money mysteriously and then he changed. So have I."

"Perfectly natural," Alexi soothed. "I once thought I was in love, but the spark disappeared even despite her beauty."

"For us, we drifted apart. He demands *pure love* which I cannot give to him. Maybe a man such as you could incite me to give such love with emotion."

She felt rather than heard Alexi's response as he pulled her into an embrace. Heat emanated from his exotic body. It was all she could do to distance herself enough to think clearly.

"Tomorrow I am driving to our beach house, less than an hour away in a deserted area. Would you like to join me?"

He wrapped a strong arm around her lower back and pulled her to him tightly. "Perfect plan. I will take the day off!"

"I will pick you up at the end of the alley where we spoke earlier."

Details dispensed, Heleanne allowed the wash of emotions to flood her senses. Accompanying the pulse of passion was a thrill of accomplishment.

She took the time to memorise the feeling of his chiselled torso against her own body before pressing him away and turning towards home.

But only three steps later, she spun back, facing Alexi. "Is it true you are an assassin?"

He only smiled enigmatically. "Let's talk about that another time, gorgeous lady."

Her heart pounded in her chest, but Heleanne maintained her poise and walked away. She could still feel his eyes upon her though. When she reached the distant gates of home, she turned to see Alexi still in the same spot, staring after her. But a split-second later he had vanished, almost as if she had imagined him.

Three

The summer house stood proudly on top of a small hill. Heleanne leaned against the white wall next to the blue door, staring down to the small bay below where turquoise waters lapped against the white sand.

She could still feel the swell of Alexi's bare chest where she had laid her head some ten minutes earlier.

"Our seventh-day anniversary," she had whispered to him. "No one touches me like you."

As if she had given him a playbook, he had traced his fingers delicately over her skin, causing yet another thrill to race up and down her spine.

"I am falling in love with you," Heleanne admitted. "But is getting harder to come out and meet secretly. Valentino is watching."

"Let him watch," Alexi's husky voice replied. "I feel the same for you. Not just your beauty, but all of you. I fear you have captured my soul."

Her pulse pounded in her ears. "Can you imagine us together?"

"I can," he said breathlessly. "If you do not mind living in my caravan."

"But we could have the big house and my husband's wealth," she spoke thoughtlessly.

"No court in this country would award you your husband's possessions if you divorced him."

That's when she had raised herself slightly so her breasts dangled temptingly in front of his face. "But there is always another way. Isn't there?"

With a chuckle he took the bait and began caressing her bare chest. "What is your foxy mind thinking of?"

Heleanne did her best to block out the sensation of his hands which had the power to drive her wild. "The first day we met, you made it very clear. And that old woman said you provide all kinds of services."

"You'll have to be more specific, you gorgeous fox." Then Alexi attempted to distract her by employing his lips as well.

Heleanne had pushed him away. "Don't play dumb with me. You know which other way I mean."

Alexi took her coolness in stride. "I said you will have to be more specific, Heleanne. Like you were when guiding me where to kiss you, and how you wanted to be touched. You had no problem being specific then."

Heleanne had glared into the depths of those brown eyes, ready to measure his upcoming response. "Simple," she said. "You assassinate my husband and we can be together. No hiding. No caravans. No poverty. No secrets."

His nostrils had flared. "You know this is not a joking matter," he huffed. "I am in love with you. I would be glad to see the last of your husband."

Silently, she watched him another full minute.

"Then do it," she said. "We both want the same thing. You do it."

Only a quick squint of his eyes betrayed emotion. Otherwise Alexi remained silent, almost challenging her to continue.

"I will invite you to my home, and give you small repair jobs so you can get to know the house and its rooms."

"No good," Alexi responded immediately. "Your home is guarded by dogs. I must catch your husband outside somewhere."

"He rarely goes out," she sneered. "All day he either reads or writes. Or meddles with the cooking."

Alexis remained silent.

"What?" she asked. "Are you scare to do it? Do you have doubts?"

He had fixed his gaze on hers. "All I need to know is that you are sure." His voice was stern.

"Well." She took a shallow breath. "I am not really sure. It was just a thought."

"You should not play with such matters." And with that, he had risen from bed and availed himself of the luxurious shower while Heleanne dressed and made her way outside for fresh air.

She heard him now, probably tossing the towel carelessly on her bedroom floor, putting on his clothes. Soon he joined her outside the beach villa.

"We cannot meet here tomorrow," she instructed. "Valentino rented out this house for the next three months."

"Then I will come to your place in town," Alexi offered.

"No."

"But my heart will explode if I do not see you."

"Well, maybe," she relented. "Just not in the daytime. He and I have separate bedrooms."

"I cannot live without you. To see you, to touch you… to sniff your scent."

"Ha," she scoffed. "Let's see if my assassin can get things done."

"I can," he assured. "But you need to make up your mind. Give me any test, as long as it will lead me to you."

Her eyes flashed. "Tonight then." Her voice rose defiantly. "My window will be unlocked. You will need to overcome the guard dogs somehow to join me."

"Put a white scarf at your window." Alexi shifted to stand in front of her, placing both hands on her upper arms. His grip was firm but not controlling. The smell of his fresh skin was almost intoxicating. "Close it there, half in and half out. I will come."

Heleanne struggled to maintain control. "There are four killer dogs," she reminded. "If they catch you, they will shred you to pieces. But while they are being fed in the kitchen, you should have five full minutes to make your entrance. Then the same thing in the morning. Valentino keeps them on a rigid schedule."

Alexi's voice grew husky. "That sounds like an invitation to spend the night with you. For that, I would swim with crocodiles, never mind four dogs."

Heleanne felt all resistance vanish under his touch. Her lips sought his, and she found her match. Time stopped under the Mediterranean sunshine as they made love in the courtyard under the branches of an ancient olive tree.

Afterward, she gazed down once more into Alexi's eyes. "You still need to prove yourself," she purred. "It is the only way for us to be together. We'll have wealth to enjoy life… maybe even have children before I grow too old."

Alexi lifted them both to a seated position and cupped her face between his hands. "I was hoping for the exact same thing. I knew this was what you wanted." She saw his Adam's apple bob as he dry swallowed. "But this cannot be a paid job, my gorgeous lady. Do not go to the market offering payment. It will mess things up."

"So it is true then," Heleanne whispered. "You are assassins."

Alexi's expression grew subdued. "No comment. Yet I can scope out your house tonight… *after* we enjoy each other in your bed!"

Heleanne's laughter peeled forth. "My darling, you already took your payment in advance!"

Four

That night after two hours of quiet passion, Alexi dressed and donned short boots with soft soles. "Give me a lucky kiss!"

Heleanne was physically and emotionally spent. But his words forced her mind back to their secondary purpose. Her lover was going to scout things out for their future. "Remember, the door with the glass knob."

Nodding his understanding, Alexi made his way into the corridor, closing the bedroom door silently behind him. Halfway down the hall, he heard the sound of canines sniffing as if they'd already caught his scent.

Scanning left and right, Alexi's eyes were drawn to the room with the clear doorknob. From behind that came one low growl, followed by others. Perhaps several of the dogs had been invited to join their master that night.

Instantly, Alexi retreated to Heleanne's room. To his horror and surprise, however, her door was now locked.

He jiggled the handle a second time and contemplated knocking when the sound of the dogs next door escalated from growls to mad barking. Alexi made a dash down the stairs and didn't stop running until he'd reached the safety of his caravan.

⸻ ◇ ⸻

The next day Heleanne made her way through the marketplace. As she passed the gypsy stall, she motioned for Alexi to follow her.

At their usual street corner, she confronted him. "You are not a real assassin. It was all just talk."

"He had dogs inside his bedroom," Alexi countered. "I came back to your room, but you had locked the door on me. What else was I to do? Your husband must suspect something."

"He is not stupid," Heleanne spat. "And I always lock my bedroom door. I do not want him surprising me whilst I am asleep." After a short pause Heleanne clutched one of his hands in hers. "I did hear at least two dogs barking in the gardens, though. What happened? How did you escape?"

"I always have a back-up plan," Alexi told her with pride. "My buddy was waiting outside. When I signalled him, he made noise to attract the dogs so I could get safely away."

"Still. You didn't do the job," Heleanne tormented.

"Can't be done in your house," Alexi insisted. "Especially if he suspects something."

"He rarely goes out," Heleanne reminded. "We haven't slept together for years now, and we barely even speak." Her will was on the verge of collapse. How could someone get to her husband in a way he wouldn't expect? "I know," she snapped. "Do you have a girl assassin?"

"We do…" Alexis said. "But she will want to be paid."

"Valentino is sex starved. He likes younger girls. If you have a good-looking girl assassin, she can flirt her way into his bed. Then the job can be done inside the house."

"All our girls are pretty, and experts in pleasure. You have the mind of an assassin! But it will cost you."

"How much?" Heleanne asked.

"Our master determines the price. But the old man is unhappy because he knows about us."

"Why does he know about us? I told you no one must find out."

"I kept disappearing for days. He is not stupid. The master will demand some kind of payment."

"I don't have any cash," Heleanne pouted.

"He prefers gold and diamonds anyway."

Her eyes swirled at the thought. "Gold, I can get," she confirmed. "And diamonds."

"Payment in advance," Alexi winced.

"Okay. You arrange it and I will find the jewels." The gears started turning in her mind. "I cursed at the maid yesterday and she did not show up today. Why don't you bring your girl assassin and I will recruit her to replace our housekeeper? Curvy and young, but not too young. She can flirt with Valentino. Gain his trust. Then she can lure him anywhere to kill him."

"That might take too long. She could simply kill him inside the house. We have a special poison that disappears from the system in twenty-four to forty-eight hours. All you have to do is delay your announcement of finding him. The death will be classified as due to natural causes."

"That is good. We don't want anyone to suspect me of poisoning him." Heleanne licked her lips and thought for another second. "Why don't you bring me some of that poison to stock, just in case."

"Why," Alexi chuckled. "Do you have someone else you want to get rid of?"

Devilish thoughts spun at the back of her mind. "No! Just in case I have to do it myself. But what about the dogs? The police will not believe an assassin got past them. Your girl will have to take the fall, or else the finger will be pointed at me."

"Easy. We'll poison the dogs, too. Then they'll think the assassin definitely came from outside!"

"Clever." She took a slow, deep breath. "That way no one will suspect me."

The two stepped close together for a passionless kiss. Having a plan should have made Heleanne more confident, but instead, worry nagged her worse than ever.

"Your assassin must not know I am involved. If she is caught, she might tell."

Alexi seemed unconcerned. "We assassins never reveal our clients. It is part of our code."

"Still…" Heleanne said apprehensively. "I'd rather she did not know."

"You're the boss," he nodded. "Just get the gold and diamonds ready. Come past our stall before mid-day and walk by the caravan that has the red flag. I will be there with Baba. But I must warn you not to bring forgeries. One false step and he will send you away."

"Okay, okay!"

"And negotiate," Alexi coached her. "Do not just give in to the price he wants immediately. Make him haggle a bit. But be ready to pay what he wants. He may reject certain jewels, so have something extra that you're wearing."

At last Heleanne exhaled. "That's a game I'm well skilled at…" As she turned away, she added under her breath, *"The game of getting men to feel like they've got the better deal."*

Five

Helanne drew the scarf tighter around her throat and adjusted her sunglasses. The sky held just a few small scattered clouds, which the wind was blowing around. She made her way through the bazaar, past the gypsy stall to where several caravans were parked. Identifying the one with the red flag, she made her way elegantly through the open door.

Alexi was standing in wait. The one he'd referred to as Baba was there, too, with grey-black hair and a short beard. Contrary to her expectations, he was dressed immaculately in a black pinstriped suit.

The older gentleman examined Heleanne from head to toe, finally fixing a hard gaze into her eyes.

"Remove your scarf and sunglasses." The instruction had come from Alexi.

She did as requested.

The man continued his examination. "Indeed pretty. No one would expect a devil behind your angelic looks."

Shaken, Heleanne looked to Alexi for help. "Consider it a compliment," he soothed.

Then the old man lapsed into some sort of Gypsy language. Heleanne felt sure he did not trust her.

Alexi replied to Baba without concern. "She is frightened, that's all. She would die for me, and I would do the same."

Heleanne nodded vigorously. "I never did this before. I only agreed to meet you because I trust Alexi with my life. I would give anything to be with him."

Baba's tone was sarcastic. "Oh yes, stricken by Eros's arrow."

Heleanne's voice came out in a squeak. "But I do love him. I would do anything for Alexi."

The old man flashed her a stern look. "Then why not just walk away from your husband? Simpler, yes?"

Bewildered, Heleanne again looked to Alexi for help, but this time he did not speak. The silence crowded in on her, so she blurted, "But how are we going to live? How can we support a family? Children?"

Baba clasped his hands together and steepled his fingers. "Children grow healthier in our caravans than those prison houses in which you live."

"I put up with Valentino all those years. I am entitled to the house and his cash. I have wasted enough of my life sitting in that golden cage. When he dies it will be mine anyway. But I want Alexi to share everything with me."

Baba's silent glare bashed against Heleanne's resolve. The silence lasted for over a minute.

In desperation she said, "He will die soon anyway. The future belongs to me and Alexi!"

When another long minute had passed, she burst into tears.

Between sniffles she choked out the words, "I am willing to give up everything for Alexi... if that is what he wants. But it would be unfair. We have a right to enjoy ourselves. And we could help you and the others. We could buy you new caravans. Bigger, more comfortable. My husband has lots of money. Millions!"

Alexi turned towards her with surprise in his expression.

"That is what I was afraid of," declared Baba. "You want it all and you are willing to do anything to get it. That makes you a very dangerous woman. I fear Alexi has been blinded by your beauty."

Heleanne's jaw fell slack. When she recovered, she lashed out at Baba. "Alexi is no less handsome than I am beautiful. We are a perfect match."

"True, but crocodile tears betray your unloving character."

Heleanne drew herself up to her full height, sniffled once more, then instantly the tears stopped. "Alexi, my darling. Your baba already has his mind set against me. Say something."

Alexi reached out and squeezed her hand tightly in his, but remained silent.

Baba said more in their shared gypsy language that Heleanne could not understand. But she felt tension course through Alexi as his hand went rigid inside hers. She could tell that whatever the old man was sharing, it was not good, and judging by the look on Baba's face as he punched the air with both fists, any hope she had at negotiating a bargain was already lost.

Alexi took a breath to comment, but Baba continued in that strange tongue.

Finally there was a pause and words tumbled out of her lover's mouth that shocked her with their depth. "Heleanne is one of us now. She is my woman. Once she is free, we will get married. We will throw the biggest gypsy wedding party ever." Then he added in a softer voice, "I trust her with my life."

Unconvinced, Baba shook his head.

Alexi was now eager to please. "Remember, the real payment is her husband's wealth. Millions will come to my hands. I mean… *our* hands!"

Baba once more lapsed into gypsy-speak, and even Heleanne felt the dagger edge of his words press first against her throat, then her chest, as if tightening around her heart to squeeze the very life out of her.

Exchanging a glance with Alexi, she found her voice once more. "I am the one who is in danger. You could report me to the police and tell them what I have asked you to do. Or you could wait and tell them after the assassination… which would send me to prison for life."

Baba nodded, his fingers once more steepled beneath his lips.

"Since you lot are assassins," Heleanne continued, "how do I know you won't turn on me after I marry Alexi, just to get your hands on my inheritance? The way I see it, I am the one who is risking all."

Baba arched a single eyebrow. "I suppose that is an option."

"That will never happen!" Alexi yelled. "We have our code of honour. You will become one of us. Everyone will have a duty to protect you."

Baba shook his head gravely. "The risk is on your head, Alexi. You knew the rules. We do not get involved with clients. Worse, you have fallen in love with this snake who has no such code… which is even more dangerous."

"I am not a snake," Heleanne protested. "I am a very good person."

"She was not a client when I fell in love with her," Alexi defended. "The job came after."

"Ach," conceded Baba. "That was the only reason I even considered this meeting. But are sure who is the target?"

Heleanne looked to Alexi in disbelief. "What is he talking about?"

Apparently feeling more in control now, Alexi squeezed then released her hand and motioned for her to calm down. "Of course I'm sure. The target is her husband. She hinted that from the first day she came to the market."

Baba looked dismayed. "You bypassed the rules of engagement."

"He visited our stall at the bazaar and bought the pink juice. I saw him. Nothing special. Nothing to be concerned about."

Baba once more narrowed his gaze on Heleanne. "Who is your husband?"

"Valentino," she replied indifferently.

"Who is this Valentino?" Baba's voice raised. "Where does he come from? What does he do? Is he a criminal? Does he have a family other than you? Does he have the money you claim he has?"

Feeling more confident now, Heleanne sighed. "He is retired, but he has investments. No family that I know of. He's from somewhere in the north and he never talks about his past. Just a boring loner."

Baba did not look amused. "Loners have a life. And a past. Secretive people can have especially dangerous pasts."

"Not this one." Heleanne's lower lip extended in a pout. "All he does all day is read, write and train his dogs. Sometimes he cooks when he wants to get under the maid's skirts. Nothing of interest, I tell you. Probably a lonely, spoiled child who inherited his wealth."

Pointing to the table Baba said, "Let's see the gold."

Heleanne opened her handbag and placed a bracelet on the table.

Silently Baba waited.

She glanced to Alexi then reached again inside her bag to retrieve three pearl neckless.

Baba pushed one of them away immediately. "Lady, you are insulting me. No games. Place all the gold on the table."

Alexi nodded encouragement for her to continue, so Heleanne pulled out a small velvet bag and emptied its contents onto the table. Three gold rings, each with a small diamond, and one white gold one, also containing a slightly larger diamond, now lay before them.

"And those are real pearls," she pointed with consternation.

Baba just shook his head.

"Valentino bought me this. He told me they were real… and *very expensive.*"

A ray of sunlight flashed through the heavy blinds, as if providing illumination to her thoughts.

"That cheap bastard," she mumbled. Heleanne removed the diamond ring from her right hand and placed it on the table.

When Baba brushed a hand through the air, she feigned reluctance before taking off the one-carat diamond ring from her left hand.

Still he maintained his vigil, waiting for more. She reached behind her neck to unclasp her necklace with a diamond pendant, placing it beside the pile amassing on the table.

Once more Baba shook his head. "You want my girl to risk being seen, but you bring only peanuts. Peanuts are for monkeys, not assassins. Take your trinkets and get out."

Heleanne had to react quickly. "This is all I could get now. If I asked my husband to open the safe for me, it would have raised suspicions." She had also risked so much. How much further would she go? "Consider this a… down payment?"

Baba's voice was stern. "I will want as much more just for half the down payment. We do not give credit! The other half we will take from the safe afterwards, so you better pray it has enough to cover your debt."

Panicking, Heleanne's hand returned inside her bag. She wrapped her fingers around the large blue velvet box. Opening it on the table to display the sparkling necklace with a gigantic diamond surrounded by emeralds, she sighed. "This is my last piece. I had the gemstones verified by a reputable jeweller. The central diamond alone is worth over one hundred thousand. If this is not enough, then I have no more."

"That is more than enough to cover the full payment for the job," Alexi intervened.

Baba still seemed unhappy. "This will cover the down payment," he acquiesced.

Heleanne let a soft smile form on her face. "Agreed. Then the rest when you open the safe."

As soon as Baba scooped the jewels into a container and whisked them away, Alexi began his questioning. "Joline is away. Who are you thinking to assign the job?"

"This will require patience and charm. It is not a job for Joline," Baba muttered. "Holly Ann would be best. She is also the only one available right now. Unless you want to wait."

Heleanne could feel her heart pounding out of her chest. "No wait. The sooner the better. Our maid just left us so there is a vacancy. This will be the best opportunity to get her in the house before he hires someone new."

Finally Baba nodded. "Tell us when she should come to your house."

"Right now," Heleanne suggested impulsively. "I will pretend I found her by the gate asking to tell my fortune, then begging for a job."

Baba's eyes narrowed. "You are too eager. That is always more dangerous!"

"Valentino never advertises. He already asked other maids for recommendations."

Baba sighed. "Holly Ann it is then."

Alexi's spirits seemed to raise. "Even better. He has seen Holly Ann at the bazaar. She's the one who sold him the Assassin's pink juice. I believe she has him charmed already."

"The girl with the scar on her face?" Heleanne recollected. "That's even better, because Valentino does not like strangers. Tell her not to wear lipstick or makeup, and to dress simple but clean."

She didn't notice the exchange of glances between the men, but did hear Alexi's muted plea. "She loves me, Baba. For the first time in ages I feel love for a woman again!"

The old man merely patted Alexi on the arm. "This will all be on you, child." Then he moved to the door and ushered them both out, saying, "Mid-day, Holly Ann will be waiting outside your gate."

Alexi grasped Heleanne by the arm and practically marched her down the nearest alley before pressing her against a cold stone wall. "I told you to hold back and bargain. You gave him too much! That necklace would have been more than enough for the whole job. Now we have no choice but to pay even more."

"I can renegotiate," Heleanne countered.

"No, now he knows you have it. You cannot change your mind. Not now… or ever."

<h1 style="text-align:center">Six</h1>

At precisely noon, Holly Ann met Heleanne outside her house. "You have been briefed what to do?"

Holly Ann nodded.

"Then let your hair down. My husband is a sucker for long, black hair."

They gypsy woman did as requested and the waves of her dark locks cascaded well past her shoulders.

Heleanne led the way into a large kitchen where Valentino was preparing his lunch. "I knew I could find you here. You get your headaches if you don't eat on time."

Valentino didn't turn from the stove or even acknowledge her presence. Two guard dogs rushed to the door, however, catching scent of something beyond the ordinary.

"I've brought a new replacement maid," she said. "We will try her for a few weeks to see if she's any better than that lazy and dirty beggar you brought last time. You know, the one who ran away without giving notice."

This time Valentino cast a hasty glance over his shoulder, but upon seeing the gypsy's presence, his entire expression morphed. First it was a look of pleasure, almost longing, but quickly Heleanne saw him tamp that down, perhaps so she wouldn't know how pleased he was with her choice.

"I see you brought the assassin," he said coolly.

Had Heleanne miscalculated? No, impossible. She'd seen the momentary desire there. He was just playing a game now. Wasn't he?

Holly Ann's face beamed radiantly as she swept inside, greeting the dogs as if they were her pets rather than vicious killers. "I already told you we are merchants. Those products tags are just good marketing."

"Of course," replied Valentino, now almost mesmerised by the gypsy woman. "I remember well. You sold me the Assassin's pink juice, promising the world."

Heleanne relaxed. He appeared to have accepted her already.

"You did not return it," Holly Ann noted. "It must have lived up to its promise."

Valentino once more stirred the pot on the stove, stalling. After half a minute he set the spoon down and stepped directly in front of the gypsy. "Funny enough, it has. I can now empty my bladder fully. It even eliminated the need to wake up at night for that function."

Holly Ann's smile beamed. "Then I will bring you more tomorrow."

"Very kind of you," Valentino nodded. "It will save me a trip to the market. I was not sure you would still be there."

Heleanne smirked. The gypsy caravan had an extremely lucrative reason to remain in this town, at least until her contract with them was completed.

Valentino returned to his cooking. "Have you tried the juice yourself, pretty girl? Has it refreshed parts other juice cannot reach?"

Heleanne shook her head. So like her husband to turn the conversation to sex.

Holly Ann's laughter tinkled. "My parts do not need any juice in order to be refreshed. But I do find it relaxing for me."

"You have a childish sweet smile and laughter. That indicates a good loving heart," he observed.

Lifting her head high, Heleanne barked, "You sure don't lose any time. Already flirting with the help. Holly Ann, you must watch out for this one. Don't fall for his false charms."

With a confident tone Holly Ann's gaze never left Valentino. "I have never misdiagnosed someone's character. It is a gypsy gift we carry in our DNA. I believe this man has a soft heart. He has much love to give."

Apparently her husband enjoyed watching this gypsy creature contradict her. His lips sealed in a genuine smile.

"Mr. Valentino is gifted with both good spirits and handsome looks." Holly Ann was certainly unleashing her charm now. "And his smile is so genuine. I think he is very rare man."

It infuriated Heleanne that this woman could read her husband's expressions. "Don't forget why you are here. To clean and work, not flirt at the first opportunity."

"I do apologise." Holly Ann turned to her. "If it came out as flirting, that was not my intention. I just described what I have seen." On that final phrase, the gypsy returned her full attention to Valentino.

"Nice!" he hooted with laughter, glaring at Heleanne. "You found someone who is not afraid to tell you the truth." Then he turned off the stove and moved to stand between the two women, but now facing the gypsy girl. "You tell the truth and we will get along fine. Do not be afraid of the blonde snake. And no matter what she says or does, do not run away like the last one. You will work for me… not for her."

Heleanne wanted to scream. *Blonde snake.* The blood coursing through her veins ran cold.

"Thank you, sir," Holly Ann replied demurely. "I assure you, you will only hear the truth from me."

"Marvellous." Valentino raised both brows as he asked, "And what shall we call you, young lady?"

"The old hag told you at the market, and I said it just moments ago," Heleanne mocked. "Weren't you listening? Her name is Holly Ann."

"Ah, but if I remember correctly, your real name is Rafaella."

Surprise filled and warmed the gypsy girl's face. "You have a very good memory, Mr. Valentino. However, everyone calls me by my nickname, Holly Ann."

Heleanne observed her husband's face droop, but almost as soon as she noticed the change, the gypsy woman continued.

"You though… you can call me by whichever name pleases you."

Heleanne wasn't sure in that moment whether to love or hate the magic that woman possessed. It was surely working full strength on her husband.

Valentino went to the sink and dried his hands on a kitchen towel. He returned to Holly Ann, taking her right hand, and flashing her a charming smile before lifting those fingers to kiss the backs of them. "Indeed, you tell the truth, and you mean what you say. That is a rare gift some can never possess."

Heleanne felt the barb even before her husband punctuated that last sentence with a hateful glance in her direction.

"You are a gifted girl," he continued to Holly Ann. "Warm of heart, truthful, intelligent, beautiful… but even more important than beauty, you have a warm sweet smile. The best gift a woman can have."

"Empty words," drooled Heleanne. "You are full of them today."

Holly Ann smiled politely. "Thank you for the compliment, sir. Shall I take it then, that you agree for me to work in your household?"

"I don't need his agreement. This is my decision," shot Heleanne. "He cannot sense good character. The last one he selected ran away. And she wasn't the first."

Her husband resumed his meal preparations, apparently unfazed.

"I am going now, sir," said Holly Ann. "If you agree, then look out your window for me at mid-day tomorrow."

Placing his meal on a plate, Valentino replied, "I rarely look out the window. I don't have such time to waste." Then he turned, holding the dish. "Even if you are out there, what will I benefit? You will probably change your mind once you realize how many other girls have run away from my wife's poison."

Holly Ann simply bowed her head slightly and bid them both goodbye.

When the girl was out the door, Heleanne faced off against her husband. "You do not miss an opportunity. From the very first moment, you started flirting with that girl. Remember that she is here to work… to cook and clean. *Not* for your pleasure."

The words seemed to have the proper sobering effect on him, but Heleanne began to wonder if watching this assassin seduce her husband might be more pain than pleasure for her as well.

Seven

The next day, as the sun crept high in the sky, Valentino stood at his office window gazing out. He scanned the area, but no one was in sight.

He chuckled to himself then said, "Fooled by a beautiful gypsy girl! She's done a runner before she even started."

"I always keep my promises and appointments, sir." The sweet voice came from behind him.

Valentino spun to find Rafaella smiling, garbed in a beguiling and colourful dress and clutching a small bag. Behind her trailed two of his dogs, relaxed and panting at her side.

"You are here," he observed with amusement. "Fooled twice in one day." Satisfied, he walked behind his desk and sat.

"The other maid directed me to your office. She is cooking for you now. I will get acquainted with the house and the jobs. But first..." She placed the bag on the desk before him. "I brought you another bottle of our Assassin's pink juice. This one is on me. My lady already charged you double anyway."

"You are a generous girl," he said, as if assessing her in a new light. "Thank you."

As the gypsy woman retreated from his office, Valentino pulled out the juice bottle and smiled to himself.

Days passed more happily for Valentino. It seemed there was never a boring moment. Whenever he concluded the office tasks—monitoring his investments, corresponding with various solicitors—he could look forward to seeing Rafaella somewhere around the house. And indeed, he did.

Today she was in the kitchen, preparing some exotic food that smelled sinfully delicious. Again, two of his dogs lolled at her side. Apparently she had made friends with all of his fierce canine protectors.

He sat at the small table in the kitchen rather than wait in the large and lonely dining room. It was a pleasure just to be near this woman who hummed merrily while she worked.

Valentino took joy in watching how precisely she placed his meal upon the plate, how each item was arranged to be as enticing as it was tantalising to the taste buds.

Rafaella moved with grace as she set the meal in front of him. The dogs heeled themselves next to their master, one to each side of him.

He cut two fragments from the tender chicken dish and tossed them the morsels which were gobbled up immediately. Then the dogs lay at his feet, seemingly content.

"You have ingratiated yourself to us all with your charm and fine cooking," he praised, resting the knife and fork back on the table. "Please, sit with me."

"I couldn't," Rafaella refused demurely. "There is still much work to do."

"I insist." Valentino rose and pulled out the chair opposite him, waiting for her to step into position so he could assist by pushing the chair back in for her in a gentlemanly fashion.

"I'm not sure your wife would approve of me sitting down on the job, sir." Rafaella's voice had a melody unto itself.

"Heleanne has gone off to town, as she usually suits herself these days," he confirmed. "You needn't worry about her."

Rafaella smiled demurely. "Ah, but a happy wife is the key to any household, is it not, sir?"

Valentino caught himself imagining what it might be like to be married to a woman who could actually be happy. To a woman more like the one seated across from him.

"Call me Valentino," he invited.

"Apologies, Mr. Valentino." Rafaella pressed her palms to the table and pushed herself up from the chair. "Does the meal not suit you?"

Valentino checked his watch, then spared a glance to both of the canines resting attentively at his heels.

"On the contrary," he replied smoothly. "Everything about you and the various talents you bring suits me."

With that, he picked up his silverware and began eating with enthusiasm while Rafaella busied herself cleaning the dishes, singing a gypsy tune in a husky alto that captivated him.

Before he had cleared his plate of the very last crumb, Rafaella was frying something else on the stove, pastries it seemed, half large and half small balls of dough. He watched as she transferred them to a platter, then arranged the dessert, forming little towers with the larger donut-shaped pastries on the bottom, then spooning cream and fresh blueberries over the lot, and topping them all with the smaller donut balls and a smidge more cream.

With great deportment, Rafaella carried the platter to the table and set it before him with a bit of flair. He gestured to her to be seated, and this time without fuss, she obliged.

"Tell me about this luscious dessert. I do not recognize it."

Rafaella licked her lips, which to him appeared equally delicious to the pastries. He allowed himself a moment to imagine what it might be like to kiss those lips, and to hear his name cried out in a moment of passion.

"It is called papanași," she almost whispered, feeding his fantasy. "But I have added my own twist to the beloved Romani recipe. Chocolate inside the dough." She reached a hand beneath the table and snapped her fingers twice. Both canines leapt to her bidding and she lavished them with attention. "So you must not feed it to your dogs."

Without missing a beat, Valentino cupped one of the donut towers in his left hand and rose from his seat to kneel in front of Rafaella, offering the treat to her for a first taste.

Again, she licked her lips. Did he see a hint of a challenge in her expression, though? But it was gone in an instant. A slow smile spread across her face as she closed her eyes and pursed her lips to receive a bite of the pastry.

Valentino stayed his hand which wanted to quiver at her mere proximity, allowing her to bite into the cream-slathered dough before pulling back.

"Mmm… delicious," she murmured. "Will you try it now?"

The left corner of her lips contained a hint of cream, and he couldn't restrain himself from wiping it away with the thumb of his free hand, brushing up against her scarred skin.

An electric jolt shot up his arm and through his whole body.

Rafaella gasped as well. It seems he was not the only one who felt the charged moment.

Leaning in towards her, his eyes returned to those succulent lips, deep red and inviting. He looked to her then, not so much for permission but rather to see if she felt the same. Her eyes had gone glassy, her pupils wide and dilated.

Valentino let the moment carry him, now longing to see if the real kiss could live up to the one he had fantasised since meeting her at the bazaar some two weeks earlier.

Their lips were almost touching. He could smell the cream now on her breath, the air stirring across his skin.

One of the dogs shifted at their feet, perhaps hoping to catch a nibble of the dessert Valentino was still balancing in one hand.

But that was enough. Their trance was broken and Rafaella pushed her chair back, instantly rising.

"I must dry and put away the rest of the dishes before your wife gets home. Happy wife, happy life."

Happy wife, happy life, thought Valentino. *If only.*

Still, he was impressed by Rafaella's resolve. Maybe he had been wrong about the whole situation. Perhaps it truly was a gift he had been given by the gods. The opportunity for a bit of happiness amidst an otherwise bleak existence.

Eight

Back inside the caravan, Rafaella felt Alexi's arm grasp hers uncomfortably. She attempted to free herself, but he was stronger.

"It's been more than two weeks now and still you haven't done the job, cousin. Why are you playing around?"

At that moment, the caravan door opened and Baba entered. "Holly Ann, Alexi," he acknowledged them. "Something wrong?"

She took the opportunity to pull out of Alexi's clutches. "I see this is no normal job. You have become involved with the target's wife. That's why you want it done quick."

"My affairs are none of your business," he rebuked. "You accepted the job. The client is pushing to have it done. If you're not up to the task, then Joline can take over."

"You forget that there are certain preparations that must take place." Rafaella's eyes flashed in anger. Your intervention is dangerous. Besides, only Baba can take the job away."

Baba clasped his hands behind his back. "I know you, Holly Ann. You enjoy flirting with the targets. You want to bed this one before you kill him."

"What's wrong with sending a happy man to paradise, rather than torturing him first?" Rafaella shook her head and those long wavy curls bobbed around her shoulders. "I explained to you both already. The target is testing his food and his drinks. He always gives a bite to his dogs first. I must gain his complete trust."

Alexi's fists clenched. "If you fail at this job, I will make you suffer a hundred times worse than any target of mine."

"Stop arguing," Baba instructed. "You, Alexi, should not be interfering. Your eagerness will endanger the job and put Holly Ann at risk."

"She's taking too long," the younger man insisted. "She enjoys toying with the husband."

"Target," Baba corrected. "You knew her style and approach before the job was assigned. Holly Ann keeps me updated daily and I approve every move she makes. Stay out of this."

Rafaella willed her breath to slow. "Tomorrow," she began. "Tomorrow I will offer to cook Assassin's pancakes for the evening dessert. No dog can sniff or taste the poison with so much honey."

Baba nodded. "What about the other maid?"

"She leaves at five o'clock every afternoon. I will use the love potion poison. His body will not be discovered until at least the next day. Maybe two, if the target's *wife* can convince the other maid to avoid cleaning his bedroom." Perhaps it was unprofessional, but Rafaella had found herself despising Heleanne.

"I will take Heleanne away for a few days," Alexi mused.

"No, you musn't," Rafaella said. "She has to be there to stop the other maid from going into the target's room."

Baba pushed a pointed finger into Alexi's chest. "Get out of here. Your mind is on the woman, not the job. You are not thinking straight. If you compromise the operation, you know what will happen to you… and your *client*."

⊷ ◊ ⊶

As soon as Alexi closed the door behind him, Baba asked, "Did you summon me only because of Alexi's interference, or was there actually something of merit?"

Rafaella tamped down her rage. "Yesterday afternoon, Valentino had the other maid massage his left shoulder."

"So the target beds his other maid," Baba brushed it off. "What concern is that to you?"

She was shaking on the inside. "You misunderstand my meaning, Baba. He has what looks like a bullet wound there." She pointed on Baba's back to the exact spot where she had seen Valentino's bullet wound exposed.

"So?" Baba remained disinterested. "Maybe he was a soldier. Maybe he got into a fight."

Next she pressed her pointer finger into Baba's chest. "And he has a small tattoo here above his heart."

"What is wrong with you today, Holly Ann?" He pushed her hand away brusquely. "Stay focused."

Undeterred, she fixed her gaze on Baba. "It is a small, yellow tattoo… *of a swallow.*"

Instantly Baba's eyes shot wide open.

Rafaella brushed a stray hair out of her face. "I'd swear I've seen that yellow swallow before, but I just cannot remember where."

Baba remained silent.

"I am sure it was *not* on a target," Rafaella continued. "I just cannot for the life of me remember who had that same tattoo."

After a deep breath Baba finally responded. "It is good you notice things. However, do not let this distract you. Lots of people have similar tattoos. Sometimes whole army units. It means nothing. Stay focused."

Rafaella couldn't be sure, but she'd swear her words had the desired effect. Now she wasn't the only one wondering about the significance of the swallow tattoo, and the man who bore its mark.

Nine

The next morning Heleanne summoned Holly Ann to her bedroom. She was standing at the window, gazing out at the landscape below when the assassin entered. "So tonight is the night."

She heard the gypsy's sharp intake of breath. "You are not supposed to know. Alexi was not supposed to tell you!"

"Of course I must know," she drawled coyly. "You will use the pure honey my husband prefers."

Holly Ann's voice did not hide her anger. "I do not need you to tell me how to do my job."

"As long as you do not mess it up. I cannot wait any longer."

Holly Ann surprised her by stomping to the window and daring to grab her arm. "Why do you want your husband killed? I've never witnessed him treating you bad nor abusing you. Is it just for his money?"

Light laughter was the only thing Heleanne spared for the gypsy's sake. "He is a softy, but do not be fooled. He has his silent ways of torturing others when it pleases him."

Holly Ann appeared to be waiting for further justification, so Heleanne added, "He smiles to everyone, laughs like an idiot, he is even incapable of telling off the maids when their service is abhorrent. But to me, he is pure poison."

"That doesn't mean he is incapable of abuse. Perhaps the way he avoids speaking to you is just his way of lashing out. It must make you very frustrated."

Heleanne felt the truth inside the gypsy's statement. A dark crevice inside her mind threatened to consume her. "You just do your job, then disappear tonight. I do not need to be preached at by an assassin."

"Alexi should never have informed you of the plans. Maybe I should change my target." The threat of Holly Ann's words hung in the air.

Heleanne flicked away the attempted intimidation. "I know of your assassin's code. If you attempt to thwart your job by pulling out or changing the plans, the rest of your kind will hunt you down and terminate you!"

But the gypsy remained equally aloof. "I can pull out anytime I like. Just the fact that you are involved intimately with Alexi is enough to justify it. Baba could even insist that I make you my target."

"You will do no such thing!" Heleanne felt the shock ripple down her spine. "I have paid a very high price. You must finish the job as planned."

"We'll see," she heard Holly Ann say before the gypsy disappeared from the bedroom. "We'll see…"

Ten

Valentino found her in the living room that afternoon, dusting the blinds and fluffing the sofa cushions.

Rafaella smiled up at him like the rays of the morning sun.

"My shopping list," he said, passing her a slip of paper. "It will take a bit of time as there are several stores you must visit. Please, do not rush to finish."

She looked down at the items he had printed on the page, visibly calculating where she must go and what must be done.

He reached into his pocket and pulled out a small bundle of cash. "Here is more than you will need, but I'd like the change returned."

Accepting the money, Rafaella finished reading the list with a look of concern. "This could take a few hours, Mr. Valentino." This extra errand in her day would throw off all her delicate timing.

"It is okay," he assured her. "There should be enough extra there for you to hire a taxi back, or to send a courier with the shopping, if you prefer."

* * *

It was early evening when Rafaella returned to Valentino's home by taxi with the shopping. Not nearly enough time to adequately prepare the meal she had planned. Never mind the dessert.

To her surprise, she found Valentino having made his own dinner arrangements.

He collected the bags from her and set them on the counter. She pressed the change into his hand. By the surprise on his face, she decided perhaps she had been more frugal than he expected.

But then he ushered Rafaella to the dinner table set romantically for two. Candles and flowers greeted her, along with the fine china and stemware Rafaella had seen the other maid polishing earlier that day.

"Tonight, my dear," he said, "I have cooked for you!"

"B-b-but…" she stuttered. "Where is the other maid?"

"I sent her out. Heleanne as well. My wife is *supposed* to be spending the night at a hotel in town with her sister, who *supposedly* refuses to set foot in my house. Stupid!"

She took a few seconds to digest this news and the implications of Valentino's various supposings. Unable to hide her surprise, she mumbled, "Perhaps you planned their exodus on purpose."

"You might say that," Valentino happily admitted as he pushed her chair in for her, always the gentleman.

"Just the two of us, then." Rafaella smiled softly as he took his seat across from her. She raised a glass in toast. "To a lovely evening."

"Absolutely," he agreed, clinking glasses. "We do not need any disturbance tonight."

"It seems maybe you have been cooking up more than just dinner." She hoped he had not missed her insinuation.

"Patience," he advised, with merriment glistening in his eyes. "All will be revealed in the right time."

Revealed? Rafaella tried to shield her concern. "Whatever do you mean?" she said lightly. "What will be revealed tonight?"

Valentino merely shook his pointer finger. "I know a few things," he hinted. "Secrets will be revealed tonight!"

Rafaella needed to recalculate her plans, buy herself time to think. Under the table her hand reached inside her small clutch bag to fiddle with the poison bottle. "I wonder which secrets you know."

"We all have to improvise sometimes."

It was almost like Valentino had read her mind. What should she do? "Indeed. Improvisation is a fine art."

After they had finished the salad course, he rose from the table and Rafaella attempted to get up to help him clear and serve the meal.

"No, sit, enjoy! This evening is for your benefit. And perhaps mine as well. Time will tell… with a bit of *improvisation*."

⁂

While Valentino went to the kitchen for their main course, Rafaella pulled out the small bottle with the love potion poison. She thought she would have just enough time to add it to his wine glass. Perhaps he would no longer be concerned about testing that drink since he had already taken a sip.

She rose and leaned awkwardly over the wide table to reach his glass, poised in position to plop just two drops.

"I hope you like…" came the sound of his voice approaching the dining room.

Rafaella fumbled to settle back in her seat before he could question her activity, frustrated and now struggling to stash the unused bottle back in her handbag.

"…beef bourguignon." Valentino's presentation was worthy of a high-class restaurant. And the aroma! Rafaella had never been the recipient of such a gourmet meal. The tender, juicy meat lay atop a slice of grilled country bread, surrounded by scrumptious mushrooms and delicate onions and baby carrots. He had even taken the time to add fresh parsley, trimmed in tiny leaves.

She once again rose as if to help him.

"Please be seated," he insisted. "Tonight, I serve you. This may be our last meal together. You must enjoy it."

Last meal! Suspicion froze her mind and her movements. The weight of the handbag in her lap now rivalled that of a boulder.

Noticing Valentino's searching eyes, Rafaella cleared her throat. "Does this… does this mean I am to be fired? Or…"

He resumed his seat after serving them both, and again picked up his wine glass. She thought he gave it a slight sniff before raising it in his own toast. "I find all of life becomes miraculous when we treat each activity as if it might be our last. To pleasure!"

Rafaella clinked to this toast, then released the breath she had not been aware she was holding. "To pleasure…" she repeated, buying time to regain some of her composure. "Imagine. You have cooked for me! This feels miraculous enough for someone such as myself. How can I thank you?"

"Your beauty and sweet smile are thanks enough," he replied, setting down the glass without drinking, then picking up his knife and fork.

Rafaella glanced around the room. "Where are the dogs tonight?" Then realising the conclusion he might draw from her question, she added, "They almost always keep you company when there is food nearby. Happy beggars."

"Come now. You have already discerned they are my food testers." Valentino's expression was one of amusement. "But I would not poison my own cooking, would I? I fed them at their normal time and left them to snooze in my office."

Rafaella's mind spun in new directions. Had he laced her own food with poison? Was that the reason this would be their last meal? Not that they had eaten together before.

Try as she might, Rafaella couldn't tamp down her terror. What would have otherwise been a fairy tale night for any other gypsy girl had fast turned into a horror story.

She bit into the beef and marvelled at the layers of taste. "It's so tender. You must have started cooking as soon as I left." On reflection, if this were to be her last night on earth, perhaps she should acknowledge the miraculous when it made itself known. "I confess I am astonished you would take so much time and go to such effort on my behalf. You are an amazing chef, Mr. Valentino."

Her compliment was received with humility. "It's nothing compared to your cooking," he replied. "You cook with passion. Your meals are as stunning as your beauty. It is as if your meals smile sweetly, like your own sweet smile."

Perhaps she could still turn the evening in her favour romantically, and accomplish not only her client's goals, but also her own. She blushed like a girl half her age. "Why, thank you, Mr. Valentino. You are full of surprises. And you have so many talents…"

"We all have our little surprises," he responded. "Not to mention our little secrets."

Eleven

Rafaella was still holding out hope that her plans might not be thwarted. "Thank you for an incredible dinner," she said, "but now it is my turn to make dessert. The most delicious Assassin's pancakes. Fresh made, with my own special love potion in appreciation of this evening."

She had only just begun to rise from her seat when Valentino came around the table and extended his hand. Cradling her handbag on the opposite side, she accepted his gesture.

Sparks coursed through her body the moment their hands met. The breath caught in her throat. She heard Valentino emit a small gasp. That was when their eyes met.

Wordlessly, he leaned towards her. Their gaze never left the other. Rafaella could feel his warm breath on her cheek. His lips parted and she could feel her own imitating in unconscious response. Her eyes fluttered then closed, willing the moment to last all eternity.

The kiss was tender and sweet. Like that of first love. It just felt *right*.

Why, oh why, was it happening this way? When had she lost control?

Rafaella pulled back, struggling to quell the waves of emotion that threatened to burst forth.

Then her eyes locked once more with Valentino. She witnessed a smouldering fire burst into full blaze. He did not hesitate. Wrapping one hand behind her neck he pulled her to him in a passionate kiss. Their lips and tongues entwined, the taste of red wine adding spice to the intimacy they now shared.

All sweetness had been bypassed. Rafaella's pulse was pounding. She could feel the press of his manhood against her hips. The thought sent her over the edge. Her free hand roamed to his lower back, clutching him into her further.

His own hand now strayed from the tangles of her raven hair, down to the exposed shoulder where the strap of her dress had fallen to the side.

"The pancakes can wait," she heard him mumble. "Close your eyes and follow me. There are more surprises tonight."

Valentino led the way and Rafaella followed without hesitation, all previous schemings about the night's mission abandoned.

In his massive bedroom, she peeked momentarily to see the bed was laden with a pure white comforter, embroidered with thread that shimmered metallic in the candlelight. One side had been rolled back to expose pale pink, silk bed linens with their matching pillows.

"Keep your eyes shut," Valentino reminded, and Rafaella clamped down her eyelids once more.

He pulled her about a dozen steps across the room before coming to a stop. The smell of roses filled Rafaella's nostrils.

"You can open your eyes now," he instructed.

She gazed in awe through the door to a luxurious bathroom with a bath capable of fitting five people, filled with bubbles and topped by red rose petals. Two wide steps led to the top of the tub.

Rafaella could not hide her delighted surprise. "Velvet red roses! My favourite flower. And how could you have guessed my dream of a bubble bath?"

"I told you, I know your secrets!"

A ripple of fear travelled up her spine, but she willed it away, wishing to live in the miraculous moment instead, relishing the gift of love that seemed to be on offer this evening.

Valentino pulled her once more into a tight embrace and this time she was the one to initiate the passionate kiss.

When his hands travelled to her bare shoulder once more, a small moan escaped Rafaella's lips, and her own fingers began to unbutton his shirt.

⁂

Nestled amid the fragrant bubbles, Valentino continued to let his hands discover all the secrets Rafaella's body might have contained. She gave not a single thought more to the one painful secret inside her handbag that now lay next to her dress in a tumbled heap outside the tub.

"I want to…"

Valentino gently set his finger against her mouth. "Please, no words. Let us enjoy this moment as if it is our last."

For long minutes they just lay together soaking in the water, tantalising each other with slow caresses, taking their time in a way Rafaella had not believed possible.

Valentino now sat opposite her, rubbing one of her feet. Her gaze was drawn to that yellow swallow tattoo. Then with a gentle strength, he drew her leg upwards, cresting the top of the water so he could lean forward and kiss her rosy pink toes.

For the first time, Rafaella saw the scar on his shoulder from the bullet wound up close. "Come," she encouraged. "Let me massage that shoulder. Does it give you pain?"

He looked at her for a long moment, perhaps assessing her motive, but finding only pure intent, he allowed her to shift behind him, wrapping a leg around either side of his hips.

She relished the moans of his enjoyment, and the way his muscles rippled under her touch. Here was no man who merely hid behind a desk all day as Heleanne had alleged.

As if she had bid the woman into the room with them, Valentino spoke of his wife. "We hardly know each other, yet you have not resisted to join me, a married man, in the bath. Why?"

She chuckled and with just the right pressure, returned to her mission to bring comfort to his aching wound. "Resist? From the first moment I saw you that day in the market, I was captured by you."

"But you must be friends with my wife," he contended. "After all, she was the one who brought you into this house."

"Hah." Rafaella couldn't help the reaction that cascaded forth. "I'm not sure your wife can have a friend. She may be pretty, but she is pure poison in my mind."

Merely speaking the word poison gave Rafaella a sudden pause. She willed her fingers to go back to their magical soothing motion, praying Valentino had not noticed any lapse.

Hoping to further draw his mind away from that slip of the tongue she added, "Tell me the truth. Your wife does not make you happy, does she?"

"You are right, there," he confessed. "But what do you expect of me? At the end of the day, I am still a married man."

"Stop," she begged. "Don't spoil this precious moment. I expect nothing of you. As gypsies, we will be on the move again. We never stay in one place for long. I would like nothing more than to enjoy your company… and your incredible touch… tonight."

"You are a rare girl," Valentino said on a sigh.

Then he rotated in the giant tub, now facing her. Rafaella shifted herself to wrap him close, her legs draped over his thighs, their chests touching.

"Beautiful, intelligent, wise…" he continued. "But cunning. You should be careful though, because truthfulness comes with a heavy price."

"Did you prepare such a scrumptious dinner and romantic bubble bath so you could interrogate me? Just ask what you want to know," she found herself offering freely. "Or I will leave whenever you tell me to. Tonight, I can deny you nothing."

Once more, she felt the heat rise from Valentino's body as he clutched her to him. "You keep surprising me, my dear sweet Rafaella. Hearing you offer, I no longer care for any of the whys. And I certainly do not want you to go."

— ◇ —

Valentino stepped out of the tub, then threaded one arm under her legs and the other around her back, hoisting Rafaella to carry her back to the bedroom.

Bodies still dripping, he deposited her gently on the pale pink silk linens. She reached up with both hands to draw him in for a magical kiss.

Time once more stood still. Their kiss was like a shared promise of what was to come. Sweet, then tantalising. Electric, then withdrawing, Rafaella scrambled to catch her breath.

Then she felt him deposit soft kisses tracing from her neck slowly south. He paused to lavish attention to her breasts, teasing the nipples into tiny peaks with his tongue, meanwhile his hands caressed the outside of her thighs.

Achingly slow, he continued his journey, pausing to kiss her belly button. She stroked his hair, momentarily pressing his cheek against her abdomen. But the flames they had stoked earlier were now fully rekindled. She pushed his head to go further down, making her unspoken desire painfully obvious.

In a sudden and surprising move, Valentino shifted his body weight and flipped Rafaella onto her stomach beneath him.

Laying his whole weight on top of her back, he once more began depositing a trail of kisses. The descent was agonizingly slow, criss-crossing her upper back, then rubbing his chest hard against her lower back.

Sliding further down, he rubbed his chest into her buttocks while reaching around to stroke her breasts. Sandwiched under him like that, she groaned in response, arching in turns to the sensations now coming from all directions.

At long last, he resumed his descent, tenderly kissing her inner thighs. But while his hands continued their torment, now teasing her most intimate region with a butterfly touch, his kisses reached the soft skin on the back of her knees. Then those tormenting hands followed his lips, providing a gentle massage to her calf muscles while his lips stayed the course all the way to the bottoms of her feet.

When she felt him slip two toes into his mouth and suck, Rafaella's cry took her completely by surprise. It was as if her entire body was engulfed in flame and only his touch could bring her solace.

Once more it seemed Valentino was reading her mind. He flipped her onto her back and now rubbed the soles of her feet, kissing his way up the way he had come.

When she felt him gently sliding his hands under her bottom, she tried to dismiss a sudden pang of selfishness. "It is not fair. I want to kiss you." But perhaps her moans of pleasure belied the truth.

"Just enjoy it," he murmured between kisses, "and let me enjoy you, my gorgeous gypsy lover."

With that, he stopped speaking altogether. He inhaled the aroma that hung musky in the air between them. She'd swear she could feel his heart pounding though only his fingertips and palms gripped her buttocks.

Suddenly kiss hungry, Rafaella knew what she would do. She pulled herself up and directed Valentino to his back beneath her. Climbing astride, she dropped her lips to his, claiming an almost violent kiss of passion.

Momentarily lost to the desire that throbbed inside her, she reclaimed self-control and threaded her kisses first to his cheek, then to his neck and ear, then down his chest.

He wound his fingertips through her long tresses, gently pulling as if to signal she should return to kiss his lips.

"My turn to punish you," she whispered huskily. "I will do exactly what you did to me."

A long, slow moan escaped his throat. "In that case," he sighed, "I surrender to you completely."

⁕ ⬦ ⁕

Afterward, they lay curled into one other, silently caressing wherever their hands could reach. "What magic have you applied on me?" Rafaella's voice was low and filled with wonder.

"The magic is all yours," he laughed lightly. "I cannot stop caressing you nor kissing you." One hand wrapped itself in the raven locks of her hair, his fingers practically memorising their texture. "You were right. It was magic between us from the very first moment."

"Ah, but I still think I wanted you first," she teased, toying with one of his nipples between her fingertips.

He landed a soft bite on her right shoulder, releasing his own fingers from her hair to clasp her nose between his pointer and middle fingers. "Temptress! Even your Assassin's pink juice has limits to how much it can restore in a man my age."

She giggled and easily brushed his hand from her nose, instead claiming one finger between her lips and suckling it.

"At least feed me first, my gypsy beauty. I'm suddenly starving, and if I remember right, you promised me some special love potion pancakes. It seems I will need them tonight!"

A sense of longing mixed with dread in the pit of Rafaella's stomach. Had she finally discovered true love in the midst of an impossible situation? Could she fulfil her role in the last scene of this play doomed to tragedy?

With a quick roll of her body, she climbed on top of him once more. "You have most certainly earned your dessert. And my love potion pancakes will no doubt prepare you for paradise, but please, stay here in bed and I will serve you like a king. It won't take but a few minutes after I have a quick shower."

"No, I do not like eating in bed," he resisted. "Bed is for sleeping. And for making love," he added, pointing to a hook on the wall near the bathroom door. "A robe for you after the shower, although you don't have to dress…"

Twelve

Exiting the bathroom wearing his robe, Rafaella blew a kiss to Valentino who was still lazing in bed.

The shower had helped to clear her head and restore her resolve. Pausing to gather her handbag from the tangle of fabric that was her dress, she had snuck the clutch past him to the kitchen, opened it and pulled out the small perfume bottle containing the love potion poison. She dropped it gently into the pocket of the robe.

Taking out another small glass bottle containing pink liquid, Rafaella drank it down. "My antidote," she whispered to herself.

After preparing the pancake batter, she retrieved the bottle of poison. She stared at the slope of the glass, noting a design etched there that signalled its contents to all gypsies without need of a label, then fingered its top with the dropper that contained the power to send Valentino once and truly… and forever… into paradise.

The bottle grew warm in her hands. As did the skillet on the stove. It was time.

But instead of using the dropper to add the planned magical ingredient to her Assassin's pancakes, she found herself retracing her steps to the counter where she had laid her handbag. She stuffed the bottle inside, leaving the zipper open, before returning to the stove to pour the first of several pancakes.

Overcome by a sense of wonder and hope, Rafaella allowed herself to become absorbed in the act of cooking this love offering. She began to hum a gypsy tune of passion and abandon as she flipped the cakes and transferred them to a plate.

So entranced was she in her song and kitchen magic that she did not hear Valentino enter the room.

He came up behind her, planting kisses on her neck while his hands gently squeezed her rear.

"Oh!" she gasped. "Do not disturb the cook, or you will get burnt pancakes! Go wait at the table if your mind is set that I can't serve you in bed."

"I think you've already served me well in bed," he chuckled, but turned willingly to take a seat at the small table in the kitchen.

But in that next moment, Rafaella saw the error of her ways. His stare was fixed mechanically on her open handbag.

He reached inside and pulled out the love potion poison, fingering the bottle in much the same way as she had moments earlier.

Then he opened the topper and inhaled. "Rose, with a touch of my favourite aroma… cinnamon."

Instantly horrified, she watched as he lifted the bottle to his mouth, ready to taste the love potion.

"No!" The cry ripped from her throat. She tossed the wooden cooking utensil towards the tiny bottle.

Yet once more that night, time stood still for Rafaella.

She watched as Valentino tipped the bottle to his lips, still maintaining eye contact with her.

The wooden utensil spun through air, end over end, its trajectory certain… but would it land in time?

Blood pounded in her ears as she waited, all choices now far beyond her control.

Perhaps Valentino had seen something in her panicked eyes, or perhaps she had merely willed the object to exceed the rules of nature in its speed towards the target.

The glass bottle was knocked from his hand and fell to the floor.

Valentino stared at her while the aroma of a burning pancake filled the air around them.

Rafaella stood cemented in place.

"It takes a lot of training to acquire the skill of throwing an object to hit your target," he observed. "Especially such a small target."

He stretched to pick up the potion bottle from the floor.

Breaking her own trance, Rafaella raced to claim it first, then poured the entire contents down the sink drain, rinsing the dregs away under running water.

Valentino merely observed her actions without speaking.

Next she tossed the bottle into the rubbish bin and brandished a washcloth which she used to soak up the drops of potion which had spilled on the kitchen floor.

Valentino remained mute, watching as she scrubbed the tile then rinsed and squeezed the washcloth at least six times before placing it back where she had found it.

Silently, apologetically, Rafaella turned off the burner of the stove. She added the single burnt pancake to the rubbish bin atop the sinister bottle.

Breaking his silence, Valentino asked, "Was that the poison with which you intended to assassinate me?"

Tears sprang to her eyes unbidden. She flung herself towards him and enveloped him in an embrace.

His body was rigid, tense beneath her. But slowly, she felt his muscles respond, and his arms wound their way around her back. She nuzzled into his neck, inhaling his scent, trying to etch every last speck of him into her memory.

Finally, her breathing returned to normal, and she raised her head. Almost imperceptibly slow, she sought his eyes. The pain that tortured her soul seemed to be mirrored in his expression.

Without a word, they kissed tenderly.

It wasn't an electrical charge this time, but rather a pulsing warmth that radiated from their lips throughout Rafaella's body. Like a mingling of their souls.

When she felt him pull away, she met his gaze once more and nodded, acknowledging the evil intent that had brought her to his home.

Wrapping his arms around her waist, without any sense of anger or betrayal in his voice, Valentino soothed, "It's okay. At least now I have experienced true love… someone who truly wanted to kiss me and be kissed by me. I am ready to die now."

A soft hiccup caught in her throat.

"Assassins never cry for their victims." With a tender stroke, he wiped the new tear from her cheek. "I would rather be assassinated by you than anyone else."

"No!" she shouted spontaneously.

Love beamed from his eyes. "I've never kissed any woman the way I kissed you. That's because I've never felt a woman kiss me like you did."

"I feel the same way," she confessed. "It was so raw and real. All the way to my core."

"You were not pretending," he said, staring into her mind and heart. "That's enough for me. True love was the only experience missing from my life. I am ready to die now."

Her hand slapped him gently. "You are not going anywhere. *You are not going to die.*"

"No woman ever made me laugh like you did, either," he revealed. "I can gladly surrender to death in your hands."

Her throat restricted. She could hardly breathe.

"I see now why they are called Assassin's pancakes!" He placed a kiss on the top of her head. "I like the idea. It is a very good and sweet way to go."

"There will be no assassination. I will die defending your life." She pulled him into a tight embrace, almost clutching him to her with her every muscle. "I will tell you all about it. And you will tell me how you knew."

"Later," he said, stroking her hair.

"Okay, then," she relented. "I still have a promise to fulfil. Let me finish your very, very special pancakes. And I will eat them first to assure you."

Refusing to release his hold, he choked out the words, "There is nothing to tell. My wife hired her new lover, but he failed, so they hired you."

"You knew all along!" She pulled back. "Why did you not try to stop me?"

Valentino smiled wistfully. "Because I fell in love with you. I suppose I wanted to see if you would really go through with it. But after we made love, I knew you would not be able to complete the mission."

Feeling restored to herself, Rafaella transferred all of the previous pancakes to the rubbish bin and began again. "No more words until after our dessert. This time you can watch every ingredient I use. And when your strength is renewed, my love, perhaps we can have something else for this meal's final course…"

$\mathfrak{T}$hirteen

The dishes were unwashed, but not a speck of food remained in evidence on either of their plates, so great was their hunger that night.

They rose from beside each other at the small kitchen table, and with childish zeal, Rafaella hugged Valentino from behind. Her arms encircled his chest, her head leaning tenderly on the back of the terry cloth robe he wore. "You are a very special man, my love. I felt strange when I first saw you at the market. I had never believed in love at first sight… but…"

A shadow fell outside the front door.

"We have guests," Valentino whispered. "Either they came for your pancakes, or to make sure you finished the job."

Rafaella's blood now thickened with terror as Alexi appeared inside the entryway flanked by Heleanne and a second male gypsy assassin who normally staffed their stall at the bazaar.

Alexi raised a knife, swinging his arm back, taking practiced aim.

With the speed and force of a boy half her age, Rafaella pressed her knee into the back of Valentino's knee, dropping him to a kneeling position.

The first dagger narrowly missed them both.

She jumped up in front of Valentino, shielding him with her body.

A second dagger whizzed through the air, thrown by the other gypsy.

In equally fast reaction, Valentino dropped Rafaella to the floor, pulling them both sideways, but cushioning her impact with his body.

The knife passed just above their heads.

Rafaella looked up to see Alexi preparing to launch another dagger in their direction. She spun her body on top of Valentino, but at the last possible second, her new lover rolled them again.

The knife stabbed Valentino just below his right shoulder.

Teeth bared, a wild howl erupted from Rafaella's lips. Fearless, she removed the knife briskly from Valentino's back, rolled him to his side, then with her other hand pulled one of the two daggers that had narrowly missed them out of the wall where it had lodged behind their current position.

She mounted a counter-attack against the two gypsy assassins. Even outnumbered and wearing nothing but a bathrobe, she was a force to be reckoned with. But with the taste of true love still on her lips, she was fighting for more than her own life.

Alexi motioned the other gypsy to move in first, while he pushed Heleanne into the dining room.

Rafaella took a defensive stance, but the moment the second assassin was close enough, she performed an acrobatic leap and stabbed him through the neck.

Blood spurted everywhere, coating her hands and face.

Alexi now moved in for the kill, while Heleanne peeked around the corner yelling, "Kill her! Kill them both!"

Her counterpart apparently had one last dagger, and judging by the look on his face, their status as cousins, as well as the many years they had travelled and trained together in the caravan meant nothing. Perhaps that night they were both fighting for what they believed to be true love.

Rafaella angled her body to block Alexi from Valentino, who was still lying on his side, blood gushing from the wound in his back.

In a sudden twist, Alexi spun a high kick that caught Rafaella in the chest, sending her crashing backwards in front of Valentino.

As she was gasping to catch her breath, Alexi tossed his dagger to the side and wrapped his hands around her neck in a strangle hold.

There was hatred in his eyes. This person she had known from childhood through a tortured adolescence to finally become a respected member of their gypsy clan had suddenly become her enemy.

Perhaps twenty seconds lapsed. The room spun then started to go dark.

Suddenly Alexi's grip loosened and his body collapsed on top of her with a heavy weight.

Valentino had struggled to his feet and swung a chair, smashing it against Alexi's back. Then Valentino dropped to his knees and clasped Alexi's hands, yanking them behind the gypsy's back in a painful bind.

Rafaella squinted, seeing astonishment spread across Alexi's features. Alexi shifted his own weight then in preparation for something she could not predict. But the pause gave her just enough time to roll away.

In the next split-second, Alexi reared his head back in a painful thrust, cracking skulls with Valentino whose grip slipped off the gypsy's hands.

The two fought bare handed for the next several minutes. Rafaella tried to manoeuvre to her feet, but dizzily collapsed. Each move Alexi made was matched by Valentino. Each attack Valentino made was countered by Alexi.

Incredulous, Alexi shouted, "How do you know our moves, old man? Who are you?"

Rafaella shook her head, trying to regain control over her balance, and take in the reality of the battle that was playing out before her.

Blood was seeping from the corner of Alexi's mouth. Valentino swayed slightly, but remained on his feet, the wound on his back having dyed his own bathrobe an angry red.

Alexi transferred the weight to his back leg and in a similar move to what had dropped Rafaella, he lashed out with a vicious sidekick that send Valentino flying backwards, dropping to his knees.

Snagging his discarded knife, Alexi positioned himself behind Valentino, one hand under her lover's chin, the other poised with the knife, ready to slice his throat open.

"Do it. Finish him!" Heleanne screamed, moving along the edge of the room toward where Rafaella still lay panting and dazed.

Rafaella knew it was now or never. With a cry of rage, she pushed herself to her feet and aimed her body at Alexi's side.

But in her weakened state, she didn't see Heleanne's foot slip out, tripping her, sending her crashing painfully back to the floor.

Alexi just laughed. "Now you will see how to finish a job!"

"No!" rasped Rafaella. In desperation she shrieked, "Take me instead! Take me!"

She thought nothing could be louder than the sound of her cousin's sinister laughter and Heleanne's primal screams.

Bang!

Then a gunshot ripped through the air, leaving the room suddenly silent.

Fourteen

The bullet penetrated the front lobe of Alexi's brain.

Rafaella's jaw hung wide, attempting to comprehend what had just happened.

Baba stood in the doorway, his arm extended, finger still gripping the trigger.

"No!" Rafaella screamed.

Her sight turned back to Valentino, her mind frantically begging that he be spared.

Bang!

A second shot shattered the night.

It was as if her heart collapsed. Rafaella folded forwards, lunging to hug Valentino to her breast.

But the bullet had not touched her lover.

Anxiously she scanned the room to determine her next move.

Alexi's body crumpled to the floor, blood now gushing from the chest wound to his heart.

Rafaella struggled to pull Valentino away from the corpse of her cousin, still hoping to shield him with her body from whatever torture might come next.

When nothing immediately transpired, she looked curiously to Baba who was still pointing his weapon.

In desperation she threw herself atop Valentino. "No, Baba!" she shouted. "Shoot me. Not him. He deserves better."

Now standing directly in front of Valentino and Rafaella, finger still on the trigger, Baba dropped his gaze on her. He stared deeply into her eyes for several long seconds.

"Shoot him, Baba. Finish the job I paid you for," came Heleanne's plea. "Then kill the girl too. The safe is here for the balance I owe you… and even more."

Rafaella watched as Baba shifted his sights from her to Heleanne and back.

In painful slow motion, he lowered the gun. "You finally found a man you will kill for," he said. "And be willing to die for. All your life you were dreaming for such a man. Your dream came true."

"I found him, Baba," Rafaella whispered, daring to hope for a different ending than the one she knew she deserved. "My wish is completed. Please do not shoot him. Shoot me instead. I beg you."

"You have broken the assassin's code," Baba continued in the same even tone. "You have not completed your job. You know the penalty is death."

Continuing to shield Valentino's body with her own, she repeated, "Shoot me. But do not harm Valentino. He cannot harm a fly. He has a warm heart."

His gaze now on Valentino, Baba broke into a joyful smile. "You think so? At your age, he was the best of the best fighters. That is, until he got shot while saving my life."

Rafaella's expression morphed to bewilderment. Heleanne appeared to be equally confused.

Baba now knelt before Valentino. "I saw you that day. You never gave me the chance to thank you."

Trying to make sense of things, Rafaella could only watch the interchange.

Baba smiled contentedly. "Finally, I have repaid my debt. No one knows your true identity. But trust me, no one will ever bother you again."

Heleanne backed away a single step, but remained inside the room.

Now looking at Rafaella, Baba went on. "It was lucky you told me of his wound, and this…" He spread open Valentino's robe to reveal the yellow swallow tattoo by his heart. "Helping me find the man who once saved my life pays all your debts to me as well. You are both free, Rafaella."

She gazed deeply at Baba while he shifted position to whisper into Valentino's ear. She leaned closer to hear.

"Our caravan is leaving in the morning," he said. "I will report the two of you dead, along with Alexi and his buddy." After a short pause, he added, "Stay out of sight. I will send the cleaners to deal with the bodies sometime late, just before dawn."

Valentino smiled his thanks and Rafaella dropped to her knees beside him. Then she reached out to clutch Baba's hand, planting a long kiss upon it.

Motion at the edge of her vision drew Rafaella's attention. Pointing to Heleanne, she asked, "What about her? She witnessed everything."

Heleanne bolted for the door.

Bang!

A third gunshot ripped through the night air. Heleanne stopped in her tracks, her eyes wide with fear. Her hands brushed over her body, trying to discern if she had been hit.

Baba lowered his weapon and strode to her side, grabbing Heleanne painfully by the upper arm. "I lost three specially trained assassins tonight. You will have a lifetime's work to repay me."

Turning his gaze on Rafaella and Valentino, he spoke more tenderly. "You have each found a bespoke heart and matching smile. Without this devil woman, your house will be a happy home."

Yanking Heleanne by the arm, Baba led her away.

Rafaella embraced Valentino, who gulped audibly but returned her hug.

"Oh, I'm sorry!" she said, pulling her hand away from his shoulder. "We have to dress that wound. Then you must tell me the story of how you saved Baba."

Valentino brushed away her concern. "It can wait an hour. First, let's eat those famous Assassin's pancakes. I'm famished, and it may take a lifetime to share all our stories."

"Pancakes, at a time like this?" Rafaella laughed.

"I thought you said you always keep your promises," he teased.

"Yes!" She shook her head then leaned it against Valentino's chest. "I will keep my promise to you and make dessert."

"And after that," he said, "you can dress my shoulder wound. For the rest, we have a lifetime." Then he leaned back and with merriment in her eyes, added, "But before the caravan leaves town, maybe you should fetch some more of that pink juice!"

Other Works by This Author

Beyond Eros (Book 1)

Aris is a successful businessman whose marriage is on the rocks. When a young, powerful woman falls in love with him, but he rejects her, she vows to win or destroy him.

Embarking on a global search for true love, Aris ventures out with two friends, risking his life in pursuit of the ancient love secret. Just as he has given up on finding true love, another woman appears. Will this love secret help Aris find his dream woman?

Is such true love beyond eros possible? Multiple evil forces, await Aris. Will he even survive to find out? Who will win Aris's heart?

About the Author

CHRIS NEO was born in Cyprus, migrated, and has practised in world-renowned clinics as a hypno-psychoanalyst. His experience in clinical love ailments gives him unique insight into the mysteries of the human heart, soul, and mind. Contrary to popular Freudian doctrine that most if not all psychological ailments derive from sex, his clinical conclusion is that most human psychological ailments derive from love, its lack, or its misconceptions.

A multi-talented individual, Neo has excelled in multiple industries, including tough business environments where many competitors went out of business. He writes for pleasure, drawing inspiration from ancient storytellers and teachers like Aristotle to more current masters like Joseph Campbell, Vogler, McKena, McKee, and others.